MERMAID ACADEMY

Dive into Magic

Suddenly a shiver passed through Lyla as she sensed a shadow moving above her. Glancing up, she saw a large shape pass overhead, swimming at the surface. Her heart skipped a beat…

For the very swishy
Sam Swinnerton.

J.S. and L.C.

To Ava Grace Lauria, enjoy
the magic and adventure!
Sending you lots of love x

L.T.

MERMAID ACADEMY
Dive into Magic

Lyla and Charm

JULIE SYKES and
LINDA CHAPMAN

illustrated by
LUCY TRUMAN

nosy crow

First published in the UK in 2025 by Nosy Crow Ltd
Wheat Wharf, 27a Shad Thames,
London, SE1 2XZ, UK

Nosy Crow Eireann Ltd
44 Orchard Grove, Kenmare,
Co Kerry, V93 FY22, Ireland

ISBN: 978 1 80513 459 6

A CIP catalogue record for this book is available from the British Library

Printed and bound in Great Britain by Clays Ltd, Elcograf S.p.A.
following rigorous ethical sourcing standards.

FSC www.fsc.org
MIX
Paper | Supporting
responsible forestry
FSC® C018072

1 3 5 7 9 10 8 6 4 2

www.nosycrow.com

CHAPTER ONE

"Finished at last!" Lyla sighed with relief as she put her squink pen down. "Thanks for the help, Mils."

"No worries," said Millie, smiling. "I know you'll help me next time I want to learn some new dance moves."

"Definitely!" Lyla agreed. "Dancing is easy. It's just words that play tricks on me."

Lyla always found reading and writing a lot of hard work, but it had been even more tiring recently. Ever since their class visit to the mangrove swamps a few weeks ago, when they'd been chased by a pair of crocodiles, she'd had nightmares. She'd even started imagining crocodiles during the daytime. Yesterday, during lunch, she had been sure she'd spotted one behind a sea fan in the Tranquillity Haven. She hadn't mentioned it to anyone, and when she finally found the courage to swim nearer and investigate, there was nothing there.

"My homework's done too," said Harper, rolling up her scroll. "Let's go and play manatee tag. Sea Jets dorm will be waiting for us."

Millie grinned at Lyla. The stakes were high. They were both in the lead, having won two games each. Today's match would be the decider! Forgetting her worries, Lyla grinned back.

"Come on, Aurora! Stop reading," said Harper, swimming over to the fourth member of Lilac Star, who was sitting on her clamshell bed with her nose buried in a book. Harper swiped the book out of her hands. "It's tag time."

"Harper, give it back!" Aurora exclaimed. "I've

only got two pages to go."

Harper waggled the book teasingly but then Millie plucked it out of her fingers and gave it back to Aurora. "Come on, Harper, let Aurora finish reading while I hand our homework in to Ms Samphire. You and Lyla find the dolphins and we'll all meet in The Singing Circle in ten minutes. OK?"

"OK," they chorused.

While Millie headed off to deliver their homework scrolls, Lyla and Harper swam out of the dorm's open window and down into The Singing Circle. Their dolphins were playing catch, and Lyla felt a happy tingle run through her tail as Charm raced over to greet her.

"Lyla!" whistled Charm, whooshing to a stop, her cheerful face breaking into a wide grin. "I've missed you. Is your homework all done now?"

"Yes, thank Neptune!" said Lyla. "We can finally head to the playpark – and beat Sea Jets!"

Charm clapped her flippers. "I love manatee tag! I've thought of a fin-tastic hiding place."

As soon as Millie and Aurora arrived, they all headed for the playpark, where the boys from Sea Jets dorm and their dolphins were hanging out by the marble statue of a manatee.

Millie and Storm volunteered to be the first pair of catchers. Eyes closed, they bobbed in front of the manatee statue, counting to a hundred while everyone else rushed off to hide. If a player touched the manatee without being caught, they won a point for their team.

"Where's your fin-tastic place to hide then?" Lyla asked Charm.

"Towards the surface!" said Charm. "In one of the caves in the coral up there. Then we can swim down while Millie and Storm are looking for the others. Take hold of my fin!"

Happy as always to go along with what Charm wanted, Lyla grabbed hold and they zoomed up through the water until they found some caves.

"How about this one?" Lyla suggested, pointing to a small cave with a direct line of sight to the manatee statue.

"No, this one's better; it's bigger," said Charm, swimming towards a cave half-hidden by a ledge of sea ferns.

"But won't the sea ferns block our view?" questioned Lyla.

Charm shook her head. "It'll be fine."

Lyla swam after Charm, but as she turned and tried to look out of the cave, she realised she was right. The ferns did block their view – she could only see half of Millie and nothing of Storm.

Millie was still counting. Parting the fronds, Lyla peeped out. Beneath them, she could see Harper and Splash hiding inside a giant vase sponge, and Nimesh and his dolphin, Swift, huddled together behind a massive brain coral.

Suddenly a shiver passed through Lyla as she sensed a shadow moving above her. Glancing up, she saw a large shape pass overhead, swimming at the surface. Her heart skipped a beat. A long blunt nose; a squat body and a very long, muscular tail; two small front legs and two slightly larger back legs…

Lyla gasped.

"Sssh!" Charm whispered from behind her. "Millie and Storm will hear you."

Lyla was too concerned to worry about the game. "Charm! I just saw a crocodile!"

"A crocodile?" Charm echoed in astonishment. "There can't be a crocodile out here, Lyla. They don't swim this far from land."

"But I saw one! Up there." Charm joined Lyla on the ledge and looked up but the shadowy shape had gone and there were just sunbeams dancing at the surface.

Charm frowned. "There's nothing there."

Lyla hesitated. She'd definitely seen something, and it had looked very crocodile-like, but Charm was right. Crocodiles couldn't live out on a coral reef in the middle of the ocean.

"Lyla and Charm! I can see you!" Millie's voice rang out.

"Oh, flippers! We've been making too much

noise and now we've been found." Charm groaned.

Lyla swished her tail in frustration. From behind the ferns, a rock jumped out, hovered for a moment and then rattled away down the coral cliff face. Lyla blinked in surprise. That was weird! But before she had time to think about it, Millie called again. "You have to come down and help us catch!"

"You were making loads of noise," said Storm, as Lyla and Charm swam to join him and Millie.

Charm's mouth opened in a wide dolphin grin. "Lyla thought she saw a crocodile." She nudged Lyla, who blushed.

Millie's eyebrows rose incredulously. "Seriously, Lyla? You thought you saw a crocodile here? On the reef?"

"I guess it must have been something else," Lyla muttered. She glanced up uneasily at the surface.

"Maybe it was a reef shark," suggested Storm.

"Yes, I bet that's it," said Millie, nodding. Reef sharks were gentle creatures and they sometimes visited the academy.

Lyla was sure that it wasn't a reef shark. After all, they didn't have four legs and long fin-less tails, but she stayed silent. Her friends weren't convinced; she must have been mistaken.

"Come on. Let's try and find the others," said Millie, swimming off with Storm and Charm.

Still wondering exactly what she'd seen, Lyla followed them.

CHAPTER TWO

Manatee tag continued, but Lyla couldn't concentrate. She didn't see the mysterious creature again but she couldn't shake off the creepy feeling that they were being watched. Every so often a bush of seaweed would sway strangely or some sea sponges would move without a current. For once she was glad when the bedtime conch rang out and it was time to head to their dorms.

"It's Sunday tomorrow. What shall we do?" asked Harper as they swam back. The reef was quieter now, the water getting darker and the fish settling down to rest for the night in caves and crevices.

"We could take a picnic lunch to the wildlife reef?" suggested Millie. "I'd love to spot a woolly seahorse again."

"Yes, let's," said Harper. "You and I can practise our magic while we're there, Millie. I'm getting much better at controlling mine but I still get tired quickly when I grow plants."

Millie nodded. "Good plan!"

All merfolk could pull mermaid fire from the rocks and learn to create a bubble tunnel to travel in. But they each also had their own special magic, which they usually discovered while they were at Mermaid Academy. Millie had been the first in Lilac Star dorm to find hers – she had ink cloud magic – and then, a few weeks ago, Harper had discovered she had growing magic.

"Maybe Aurora and I will find our magic tomorrow," said Lyla hopefully.

"That would be so swishy," said Aurora longingly.

"And I really want to bond with Jewel too."

When a dolphin and a mer bonded, their tail fins changed colour to a mixture of the mer's hair colour and the colourful patterns on the dolphin's side. Bonding made a mer and their dolphin partners for life.

Charm looked cross. "I don't understand why Millie and Storm, and Harper and Splash, have bonded but we haven't yet. I think Lyla and I are perfect for each other."

"We are," Lyla agreed. "You're great at making decisions and taking the lead, Charm, and I love helping you and paying attention to the detail. We're an excellent team!"

When they reached The Singing Circle, the mermaids separated to say goodnight to their dolphins.

"Sleep well, Lyla. I hope we do bond tomorrow," Charm said. She rubbed noses with her, giving her a dolphin kiss.

Lyla felt her heart swell. "That would be clam-tastic!" she declared.

☆

The next morning, Lilac Star ate a delicious breakfast of kelp sausages and sea potato hash browns and then each packed a lunch of seaweed wraps and kelp apples. They also sneaked in some urchin berry cookies as a treat – the dolphins loved them as much as they did!

They met their dolphins, then set off for the wildlife reef. As they weaved through the coral and swooped with the shoals of tiny zebra fish, Lyla felt light and happy. She had a whole day of fun ahead, without having to think about reading or writing.

I'm not going to embarrass myself either, she thought. *I shan't imagine any crocodiles. I'm just going to have a swishy day with my friends!*

When they reached the wildlife reef, they found a clear area beneath a giant orange sea fan. It was nestled between boulders on one side and clumps of bright-green ferns on the other. They tucked their bags under the fan and swam into the open water for a quick game of seaweed catch.

The game was so much fun, as the dolphins bopped a bundle of seaweed with their noses to send it gliding through the water and the mermaids

rushed to intercept it. Lyla had just sent the seaweed ball flying back to Charm when she glanced towards the sea fan and froze. Two green eyes were staring intently out from the shadows!

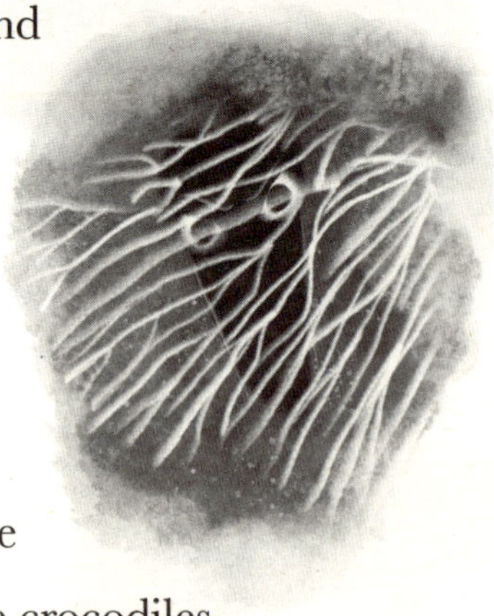

She had an instant flashback to the mangrove swamps where she and the others had been chased by the crocodiles.

Those crocodiles had had glowing green eyes. They'd been controlled by the Mal Mer, a secretive clan of merfolk who could use mind control on sea creatures to make them obey them. The Mal Mer had trapped an ancient magical turtle called Wise Sage in a cage and forced the crocodiles to guard her.

Lyla peered towards the shadows, trying to spot another glimpse of green.

"Lyla! Catch!" Harper called as a seaweed ball floated down towards her.

"One sec!" Lyla cried, swerving the ball. When she looked back at the shadows, the eyes had gone. What should she do? Maybe she should tell the others what she'd seen? *But if I'm wrong again, they'll all laugh at me*, she thought.

"You don't get crocodiles on coral reefs," she repeated to herself as she swam towards the sea fan to investigate. Her tail prickled with fear and her heart beat wildly in her chest as she dived down and peered under its lower branches. But there were no crocodiles, just some crumbling chunks of coral and scratch marks in the sand.

Relief washed over her. Shaking her head at herself for being so silly and feeling very glad she hadn't said anything to the others, she swam back to the game. Once Harper forgave her for missing the catch, Lyla really enjoyed herself, racing and spinning around with her friends as the seaweed ball flew about.

"That was brilliant!" said Millie, watching the seaweed float back down to the seabed as they all caught their breath. "I think we all deserve some lunch now, and we'll go exploring after that."

As they sat on boulders by the sea fan and ate their wraps, their conversation turned to Wise Sage. The mysterious, magical turtle travelled the oceans leaving a trail of pure wild magic that strengthened every environment she passed through, making it extraordinarily beautiful. Legend said that if she ever stopped travelling, plants and creatures throughout the oceans would fade and die.

"I wonder whether she's still in the Midnight Zone," said Millie.

When they had said goodbye to Wise Sage after rescuing her from the Mal Mer, she had told them that she was going into the deepest part of the ocean to hide. She'd asked them not to follow her and to keep her location a secret.

"I like to think of her swimming in the deep sea," said Aurora dreamily, "spreading her magic and leaving a sparkly gold trail behind her. Keeping the legend alive."

"I'm so glad we were able to free her," said Lyla. "Those Mal Mer were horrible." She shivered as she remembered their cruel faces. "I can't believe they wanted to keep her in a cage forever."

Lyla shivered. "The Malmari Ocean sounds awful. I've heard there are no wild creatures there, just the ones they keep in cages."

"The Mal Mer must have been so angry when they found out Wise Sage was free," said Harper.

"It was lucky we escaped without being caught," said Millie.

Harper, who was very good at imitating voices,

cackled loudly, sounding just like the Mal Mer mermaid they had met in the mangroves. "I'll get you, you pesky mermaids!" she said, pretending to shake a trident at them. "You'll be sorry."

"Don't, Harper!" squeaked Aurora.

Lyla caught sight of a sudden movement in the sea ferns on the other side of the clearing. She leapt up. The ferns swayed for a moment and then were still.

"What's up?" Millie asked her.

Lyla stared at the ferns but they weren't moving any more. "Nothing," she muttered, sitting down again. "I must have imagined it."

"It's all this talk of Mal Mer," said Millie, glancing at Aurora, who was still looking worried. "Let's talk about something else."

"No, let's *do* something else," said Harper. "Magic!"

They cleared away the picnic and then

Millie and Harper practised their magic. Millie demonstrated how she could now make ink clouds of all different sizes. She finished by using her tail to write "Lilac Star are the best!" in inky letters.

They all clapped and whooped.

Harper had been practising too. Now she could grow whatever plants she wanted. She flicked her tail and made pink flowers of healwort bloom all around them, then she grew two ropes of vine seaweed and made them tie themselves into a knot.

"Oh, I really wish I could do magic too," said Lyla. Aurora nodded.

"Why don't you have a go?" suggested Millie.

They both tried banging their tails against the boulders they were sitting on and waggling and flicking their tail fins, but nothing happened. Lyla gave up in frustration, slapping her tail down one last time. "It's no use!"

There was a crash behind them. They looked round. One of the boulders had toppled from its pile and gone rolling across the seabed.

"How did that happen?" said Harper in surprise.

Millie grinned. "For once, it's not one of your pranks," she teased.

Harper stuck out her tongue. "Anyway, enough work for now. Who wants a race to the giant clamshells to look for woolly seahorses?"

"Me!" they all shouted.

CHAPTER THREE

When Lyla went to bed that night, she felt the familiar sinking sensation that she always felt on Sunday nights. She loved learning but she dreaded reading and writing, and their first Monday class – Waters of the World – usually involved a lot of both.

She slept fitfully, her dreams full of fierce green-eyed crocodiles and cruel Mal Mer. She couldn't stop yawning the following morning as Lilac Star assembled in their classroom.

When Ms Samphire arrived, she was laden down with a huge box full of equipment.

She dumped it on the front desk with a thud, rearranged her jewel-studded hairband and smiled at the class. "I've an unexpected treat in store for you today. Over the weekend, Mr Nori and I visited a northern sea loch in preparation for a visit by the third-year students. While there, we discovered many new colonies of feather fish. The very subject that we're due to study this term! So today I am going to take you to the loch to look at them. The rest of your lessons are cancelled."

Excited chatter rippled through the room. Ms Samphire silenced them and continued, "Mr Nori and I believe that Wise Sage must have visited the loch in recent months, not just because of the sudden increase in feather fish but also the abundance of the wildlife we found. The third-years are going to camp there next week to study the impact of Wise Sage's visit. Your task today is to locate and mark on a map all of the feather fish colonies. The loch is vast, but if every group tackle one particular area, we should be able to complete our survey by the end of the day."

Arlo put his hand up. "How will we get there?"

"You'll travel by bubble tunnels that I will make," said Ms Samphire. "Each group will go to a different part of the loch. The loch water will be much colder than here." Ms Samphire caught the eye of Aurora and another mermaid at the back of the room and her eyes twinkled. "Those of you from Frostfin and Northstar clans are used to icy waters, but the cold may come as a shock to some of us! Amber and Maya, please hand out the explorer jackets. The rest of you get into your dorm groups and I'll come round with the equipment."

Ms Samphire swam around handing out bags with a map, a squink pen, an emergency first-aid kit and food and drinks. As she approached the Lilac Star girls, Millie automatically put her hand out to take the bag but to Lyla's surprise, Ms Samphire handed it to her instead. "I'd like you to lead Lilac Star today, Lyla."

"M… Me?" Lyla said in surprise. "But Millie always leads."

Ms Samphire smiled. "Millie is an excellent group leader but it's important that you all learn to take charge." She handed Lyla a sea scroll. "This tells you how to get to the area of the loch I would like you to survey."

Lyla tried to read words on the scroll but they danced on the page like they always did.

If she couldn't even read the instruction sheet, how could she possibly lead the group? She glanced up at Ms Samphire. "Maybe Harper could… Or Aurora…"

"No, Lyla," Ms Samphire said, her voice kind but firm. "I'm sure you'll be able to do it."

Lyla gulped. "OK," she said in a small voice, wishing she felt as sure as her teacher did.

Ms Samphire handed out the remaining bags then she clapped her hands and the buzz of chatter quietened down. "Your dolphins are meeting us in The Singing Circle. Hurry along now, we have lots to get through today."

"Come on, Lilac Star," said Millie. "Follow me!"

"Millie!" Ms Samphire nodded pointedly at Lyla.

Millie gave her a sheepish smile. "Sorry. I mean, follow Lyla, everyone."

Lyla felt very flustered. "Um… Yes… Come on, guys, follow me!"

Leading the way to The Singing Circle, she felt panic starting to spiral inside her. Oh, why hadn't Ms Samphire chosen someone else to be the leader? She didn't want to have to tell the others what to do or make decisions for the group. *Maybe Charm will help me*, she thought.

The dolphins whizzed over to meet them. "We're all going on a trip!" whistled Splash.

"To a sea loch!" said Storm happily.

"Yippee!" said Jewel.

Charm looked curiously at Lyla. "What's the matter? You don't look very happy."

"Ms Samphire's made me group leader," said Lyla miserably.

Charm chortled. "Flippers! Is that all? I thought something really bad had happened."

"It is bad. I don't want to be in charge," said Lyla.

Charm bopped her with her nose. "Don't be silly. It'll be fine. I can help you. I'm good at making decisions, that's why we make such a great team. There's no need to worry at all."

Lyla swallowed. "But it's not just the decisions," she said. "We've got a sheet of instructions of where we should go, and I can't read them. You can't help me with that, Charm."

"Charm might not be able to, but we can," Millie said, overhearing. "You don't have to read the instructions yourself. You can ask one of us to. That's what leading is. You delegate and decide who does what." She squeezed her arm. "You have really good ideas. You're going to be a great leader, Lyla."

Lyla wished she could believe her.

"Lilac Star!" called Ms Samphire, beckoning them over to the large bubble tunnel she'd just made.

“OK, everyone,” said Lyla, realising she should take charge. “Follow me.”

Millie and Aurora nodded, but Harper and Splash weren’t listening. They were trying to tag each other’s tails.

“Harper!” Lyla said, with an anxious glance at the teacher. “Ms Samphire’s waiting.”

Harper still didn’t hear her so Charm whistled very loudly. “Harper! Splash! It’s time to go!”

Harper stopped and glanced at Ms Samphire, who was starting to look impatient. “Oh.” She turned to Lyla. “You should have said, Lyla.”

“I did,” Lyla protested, but Harper had already set off towards the bubble tunnel with Splash. Reaching it, she and Splash dived inside.

CHAPTER FOUR

Ms Samphire's eyebrows were raised as Lyla and Charm hurried over. "Remember, you're in charge, Lyla," she said.

Feeling like the most rubbish leader ever, Lyla took hold of Charm's fin and they dived into the tunnel. They whooshed round in the bubbles before shooting out of the other end, gasping as they tumbled over in the cold water near the bottom of the loch. Harper and Splash were waiting for them.

Harper leapt at Lyla with a roar. Lyla shrieked in shock and Harper giggled. "Got you!" Harper shivered. "Jumping jellyfish, it's cold here!"

"But so beautiful!" Lyla said, gazing round in awe as the others arrived.

Frosty-white anemones clung to boulders that poked out among beds of dark-pink featherweed. Flame clams with fringes of bright-orange tentacles nestled among tangles of delicate brittle stars while silvery fish swam by. Lyla had never been anywhere like it. Her clan – the Sunbeam clan – lived near the surface of a warm, tropical ocean close to where a barrier reef fringed the land.

"Look, Charm!" she called, spotting a stripy blenny with huge eyes peeping at them from behind a sea squirt. She swam over to examine it.

Charm came over to look. "This place is great, even though the water's much colder here than back at Mermaid Academy!"

"It's freezing!" agreed Lyla, hunching deeper into her explorer's jacket.

Millie swam up to her. "Lyla, we should probably get started," she whispered.

"Oh, yes, of course," said Lyla, remembering that she was supposed to be the leader. Looking round, she realised her friends were staring at her expectantly.

"Do you want me to help you read the instructions?" Aurora asked. She didn't seem worried about the change in temperature at all but she came from the Frostfin clan, who lived under the ice in the Frozen Circle.

Lyla wanted to say yes but she also felt that as leader she should at least try. "I'll have a go," she said.

"You can do it, Lyla," encouraged Charm. Lyla swallowed. Charm and the other dolphins didn't come into their classroom lessons, and Lyla didn't like to talk about it, so Charm didn't know how hard Lyla found it to read.

Charm pushed her flipper into Lyla's free hand. Lyla wrapped her fingers round it. It made her feel better. Lips moving silently, she gradually worked out what the words said, grateful that none of her friends – not even impatient Harper – tried to hurry her. "OK," she said. "It says that to get to where our group is surveying, we need to find the large crab-shaped rock..."

"There's a rock like that over there!" said Harper, pointing. "I saw it when Splash and I first got here."

"When we get to it, we swim twenty tail flicks east and then head ten tail flicks north," said Lyla. Instinctively, she looked in the direction they had to go. "And then we have to record any feather fish reefs we find between that point and the shore." She looked at Harper. "Harper, why don't you and Splash show us the way to that crab-shaped rock and then I'll lead from there?"

Harper turned a somersault then grinned at the others. "Follow me!"

"You're doing really well!" Charm whispered in Lyla's ear.

For the first time since Ms Samphire had appointed her leader, Lyla felt slightly happier.

When they got to the crab-shaped rock, she took over the lead and set off for twenty tail flicks east and then ten tail flicks north. She found it very easy to follow directions, and when they reached

the area they were aiming for, she spotted a rock covered in sparkling fluffy tentacles that waved slowly through the water.

"Feather fish!" Delightedly, Lyla bent to examine them. The tips of each creature had a bright crown of orange or pink tentacles that shrank back instantly whenever the creature sensed movement in the water. Lyla and the others watched, fascinated, as the tentacles popped in and out.

"They don't look like fish at all!" said Harper indignantly, just as the sound of a small "pop" came from the rock, and in a rush of sparkly tentacles a feather fish swam out of the group, found a clear area and then stuck its mouth back to the rock with a squelch. Everyone laughed.

Lyla got the map and a squink pen out of the bag. "Ms Samphire said we have to mark any colonies we find on the map. Who'd like to do that?"

"I will," offered Aurora. Lyla handed them over and Aurora carefully marked where they were with a cross.

Lyla felt a flicker of pride that they'd found a colony so easily. Maybe she wasn't useless as a leader after all. "We need to start searching the rest of the area now."

"Should we stay together, or separate and meet back up later to report on what we've found?" asked Millie.

Lyla hesitated.

"We'll split up," Charm decided.

Lyla wasn't sure that was a good idea but it was too late. Harper and Aurora had already taken off.

"I'm going to the surface to see what a loch looks like from above the water," Harper cried.

"Wait for me!" Aurora exclaimed.

"What time should we all meet back, Lyla?" asked Millie.

Lyla groaned. She should have thought of that! The confidence she'd been starting to feel popped like a bubble of sea foam.

"Fifteen minutes?" Millie asked.

"Twenty," decided Charm.

Millie nodded. "Storm and I will catch up with the others and let them know!" She grabbed Storm's fin and set off.

Charm nuzzled Lyla. "Don't look so down. You're doing well."

"I'm really not," sighed Lyla. "I wish I was better at telling people what to do and making decisions."

"You don't need to be," said Charm. "You've got me! Shall we go after the others?"

Lyla nodded and they swam upwards, the water becoming lighter the closer they got to the surface. As they broke through it into the crisp, clear air, Lyla caught her breath. The loch was stunning! The still, mirror-like water twisted away between rocky slopes. Snow-capped mountains rose in the distance and streams of white cloud floated across the pale sky.

In the distance, Ocean Mist dorm were swimming towards a small sandy beach on the west side of the loch. There was no one else around at all. Thick swathes of pine trees clustered on the rocky land and a couple of dark boulders poked up through the still water. Lyla's gaze paused on them. They looked just like long crocodile heads. There were even bubbles coming up beside them as if they were breathing! Her heart skipped a beat. Could they actually be crocodiles?

No, she told herself quickly. You didn't find crocodiles living in lochs any more than you found them out on coral reefs in the middle of the ocean. She could imagine how much her friends would laugh at her if she mentioned it, so she decided not to say anything.

Aurora and Millie were swimming towards the shoreline with their dolphins. Harper and Splash were nowhere to be seen.

Lyla was about to suggest to Charm that they catch up when something caught her eye. Two long, knobbly heads were moving stealthily through the water from the shore towards her friends. Her heart jolted. Whether crocodiles lived in lochs or not, she knew what she was seeing.

"Crocodiles!" she shrieked. "Aurora! Millie! Watch out!"

CHAPTER FIVE

Aurora and Millie turned and saw the crocodiles. Aurora screamed and started to frantically swim away. Millie flicked her tail twice but then suddenly pulled up short. "Wait!" she shouted. "You don't get crocodiles in lochs! They—"

"SNAP SNAP!" cried a familiar voice. "I want mermaids for my dinner! SNAP SNAP!" The voice dissolved into peals of laughter.

"Harper!" Lyla cried, as Harper and Splash surfaced, long pieces of knobbly bark falling off their heads as they both shook with laughter.

"Got you!" Harper chortled, her eyes dancing with mischief.

Splash clapped his flippers. "Your faces were so funny!"

Lyla felt relief mixed with anger. When she'd seen the crocodile heads moving through the water towards her friends, she'd been terrified, and now poor Aurora looked like she was about to faint. Sharp words bubbled up inside her but she bit them back. She didn't like getting cross with people. Shaking her head, she forced a shaky smile. "Whizzing whales, Harper, I really wish you wouldn't play tricks like that."

Harper giggled, looking delighted with herself.

"It was a really good prank, wasn't it? Splash tricked me like that disguising himself with tree bark when we were in the mangrove swamps. When we saw some pieces of knobbly bark here, it reminded me and we decided to try it out on you."

Millie was frowning. "It was a clever trick, but it was also quite mean. You really frightened Aurora." She glanced over to where Aurora was being comforted by Jewel. "Are you OK, Aurora?"

"Yes," said Aurora faintly. "I was scared stiff though. I thought we were going to be eaten, and poor Jewel almost swam into a boulder."

Harper looked sheepish. "Sorry." She swam over and hugged Aurora. "I really didn't mean to scare anyone that much. I thought you'd realise crocodiles don't live in lochs. It's much too cold for them."

"It's OK," said Aurora shakily.

"Snap snap!" said Harper, nudging her. Aurora managed a little smile. Harper tagged Jewel then darted away. "Why don't we play crocodile catch, Aurora? That will cheer you up. Jewel is the crocodile!"

Jewel raced after her. Splash, Charm, Storm and Aurora scattered too.

"Wait, everyone!" called Lyla. "We should be doing our survey!" But her friends were too busy playing to listen. Lyla groaned.

"Don't worry. They'll stop soon," Millie comforted her.

Lyla sighed. "I don't know why you like being in charge so much, Millie."

She looked over to where the others were now chasing each other around the boulders. She frowned. One of the crocodile-shaped boulders she'd spotted earlier was bobbing up and down in the water. For a moment Lyla was positive she saw two gleaming green eyes blink.

She shook her head. After Harper's trick, there was no way she was going to say she thought there was a crocodile near the shore. *It's just your imagination*, she told herself firmly. But wait. Was it lifting up again…? The other one too? Lyla hesitated, torn between staying silent and speaking out.

Lyla's tail was suddenly gripped with an icy cramp and she yelped with shock. Beside her, Millie cried out. Lyla had felt the same gripping sensation when they'd been close to the Mal Mer in the mangrove swamps. To her horror, she saw Aurora and Harper grabbing at their tails too.

"Millie!" she gasped. "I think there must be some Mal—"

She broke off with a scream as two Mal Mer – a merman and a mermaid – burst out from the water on either side of her and Lyla, their magical tridents held aloft. Then two huge crocodiles with green glowing eyes reared out from between the boulders and swam at Aurora and Harper, who were swimming close by.

Lyla was engulfed by a tidal wave of panic. The two boulders really had been crocodiles! She should have said something and got everyone safely away from the area.

"Go and get help, Storm!" yelled Millie, as the Mal Mer and the crocodiles herded Lilac Star together.

Storm leapt away, followed by the other dolphins.

ZAP!

The Mal Mer shot bolts of green magic straight at the four dolphins. The dolphins' eyes instantly turned green. "Come here, dolphins!" the merman commanded them. He had short spiky hair, two jewelled studs in each ear and one

through his tail fin. The mermaid wore a silver cloak. Lyla recognised them as the two Mal Mer who had captured Wise Sage in the mangroves.

Unable to resist now they were under the spell of the Mal Mer's mind-control magic, the dolphins swam obediently to the group.

"Charm!" Lyla threw her arms round Charm, who stared straight ahead. Her friends stroked and comforted their dolphins as the crocodiles circled around them, their eyes glowing and their open jaws revealing their dagger-sharp teeth.

"Take the spell off our dolphins and let us go!" Millie said angrily to the Mal Mer, tears rolling down her cheeks as she held Storm.

The mermaid just laughed.

"Our friends aren't far away. As soon as they see what's happening they'll all come and help us!" shouted Harper. She raised her voice. "HELP!"

"Quiet!" spat Silver Cloak. She aimed her sharp

trident at Storm. "Or your dolphin will suffer!"

Harper fell silent.

Lyla looked round. Were any of the other groups in sight? No, the loch seemed empty.

"Harper's right,' said Millie. "Our friends will see us and they won't let you hurt us."

Silver Cloak's eyes gleamed nastily. "Then we'd better get you out of here."

Spiky Hair swirled his trident. A large bubble tunnel formed. "Dolphins! I command you into the tunnel."

The dolphins swam mechanically towards the bubble tunnel.

"No way! You're not taking our dolphins," shouted Harper, charging at Silver Cloak.

BANG!

A bolt of green light flew from Silver Cloak's trident and hit Harper in the chest. She shrieked and flew backwards.

"Harper!" gasped Lyla, Millie and Aurora, racing over to her.

Harper bravely tried to struggle up. "Save the dolphins!" she cried weakly.

But it was too late. All four dolphins had dived into the bubble tunnel and vanished.

"All of you, into the tunnel too," said Silver Cloak, waving her trident menacingly. "We're taking you back to the Malmari Ocean where we can question you without danger of being seen."

"We're not coming with you," said Millie angrily.

"Then you'll never see your dolphins again," hissed Silver Cloak.

Lyla looked frantically at the others. "We have to go."

They nodded. There was no way they would abandon their dolphins.

"Come on!" Lyla exclaimed, and, going first, she dived into the swirling tunnel.

CHAPTER SIX

Lyla shot out of the Mal Mer's bubble tunnel and found herself in the Malmari Ocean – a desolate, barren place, filled with mounds of dead grey coral. Bones and fish skeletons littered the seabed. A clammy feeling slid over Lyla's scales as she realised there were no living creatures here apart from the Lilac Star mermaids and their dolphins.

The dolphins were gliding along in a group, their eyes green and lifeless. A forbidding stone mansion loomed ahead, with an ornate carved door studded with sparkling gems. Light poured out of the open windows, making the surrounding ocean seem even darker and gloomier.

Hearing a rush of bubbles, Lyla swung round to see the Mal Mer and the crocodiles coming out of the tunnel too. The bubbles whirled round and then disappeared.

"Shall I dismiss the crocodiles?" Spiky Hair said to Silver Cloak. "They need to go to the surface to breathe."

Lyla felt a sudden twinge of panic. The dolphins would need to go to the surface to breathe soon too. They had to get out of here!

Silver Cloak nodded. "They have done well. Their sense of smell is as excellent as you said." She nodded at Lilac Star. "The crocodiles knew your scent from when they met you in the mangrove swamps. They've been following you ever since, which made capturing you laughably easy."

Guilt stabbed through Lyla. She'd been right

all along about seeing crocodiles at school. *I should have told the others*, she thought. *If I had told them, we wouldn't be in this mess.*

Spiky Hair swirled his trident and a new tunnel appeared. "Go back to your swamp," he commanded.

As the crocodiles' eyes returned to normal, they were swept into the bubble tunnel and vanished.

"Why have you brought us here?" Millie demanded.

"We need information," said Silver Cloak, her voice as sharp as a razor-clam. "Where is the turtle?"

"Wise Sage?" said Millie, surprised.

"Yes! Which direction did she head in when you freed her from our cage?"

"We don't know," said Millie.

"And if we did, we definitely wouldn't tell you," Harper added defiantly.

Silver Cloak gave a shark-like smile. "A spell in our dungeons should change your mind!" She flicked her trident at the front door of the stone mansion. It creaked open and she and Spiky Hair forced the mermaids and dolphins inside.

The mansion's entrance hall was vast, with many doors leading off it, each with a gold handle and studded with pearls. An enormous chandelier made from rare glittering sea gems hung from the high ceiling, and the wall panels were inlaid with mother-of-pearl. Huge golden planters filled with spiky black seaweed, and trailing sea vines had been placed around the edges of the room.

Taking up an entire wall, an enormous cage housed an animal that Lyla recognised as a spinning rainbow squid. The squid was larger than all the mermaids in Lilac Star put together. Spinning rainbow squid usually lived in the deep sea, and when they were excited they would spin

round, their arms flashing in all the colours of the rainbow. But the squid in the cage was floating forlornly, its arms glowing very faintly. It looked immensely sad.

"How can you be so cruel?" Lyla shouted, appalled.

"It's our pet now. We caught it and we're keeping it," said Silver Cloak.

"Our neighbours are so jealous," said Spiky Hair smugly. "They only have a tank of common seahorses."

Silver Cloak opened a door, revealing a long shadowy passageway that sloped downwards, lit by sconces of flickering green mermaid fire. She and Spiky Hair pushed the dolphins and mermaids through the door and herded them along the tunnel. Lyla longed to try and escape, and she could tell from the others' faces that they were feeling the same but no one was prepared to leave their dolphins.

The tunnel came to a junction and split in different directions. The Mal Mer forced them to make one turn, then another, taking them under an open portcullis, past stone pillars with vicious-looking wolf eels carved from black stone. They passed through a cave with bones littering the floor and along a tunnel where they edged past a whale skeleton then through an archway with a crack in the middle.

Left, left, right. Lyla realised there was a pattern to all the turns they were taking. *Left, left, right.* As Lyla swam on, she noticed other things, like the spotted lichen growing on the rocks, and the hole in the floor that looked like a shark had bitten it. Then, after one more turn to the right, they swam into a tunnel that ended with a wall of rough stone. There was a dungeon carved into the rock on one side. The door across it was made from bars of pale bones.

"In!" Spiky Hair commanded, pushing them forward.

"You can stay here until you tell us where Wise Sage is," said Silver Cloak.

"But we already told you we don't know," Millie protested.

"Then you'd better remember," snapped Silver Cloak. "If you don't have an answer by the time we come back, then we will take your dolphins, one by one. We have enchanted collars that will chain them to us, making them our obedient servants forever!" She laughed at the mermaids' horrified expressions.

"We'll return in one hour for your dolphins," said Spike Hair grimly. He pointed his trident at Charm. "And that big one will be first. She looks perfect for pulling a chariot!"

"No!" gasped Lyla.

Spiky Hair slammed the dungeon door shut and looked through the bars. "Then you'd better tell us where that turtle is."

"Once our ocean is restored, we can wake the sleeping beast," murmured Silver Cloak, locking the door.

Sleeping beast? thought Lyla in confusion. What did that mean? Silver Cloak handed the key to Spiky Hair, who placed it on a high ledge on the opposite wall.

"Don't bother trying to use bubble tunnels to escape," he said. "Our magic stops them from working inside the mansion."

"And even if you get out of this dungeon, you'll never get past our booby traps," said Silver Cloak. "You have one hour," she cackled, and then the two Mal Mer swam away.

Once they were alone, Harper swung round to the others. "What are we going to do?"

CRASH!

A muffled sound of thudding bricks echoed down the tunnel.

"What was that?" said Aurora.

"Does it matter?" said Millie urgently. "The important thing is getting out of here."

With the Mal Mer gone, their mind-control magic was wearing off and the dolphins' eyes were flickering between green and black. "Charm! Charm! Can you hear me?" Lyla said, stroking her.

Charm's eyes cleared. "Oh, Lyla, that was such a horrible feeling." She buried her head against Lyla's side.

Lyla blinked. She wasn't used to Charm looking to her for comfort. "It's OK. I'm here. We're going to escape,' she said, hugging her tightly. The other mermaids hugged and reassured their dolphins too.

"But how?" said Aurora, looking round their dank dungeon.

"My ink-cloud magic isn't going to be any use,"

said Millie. "How about your magic, Harper?"

"Hmm." Leaving Splash, Harper swam to the cage door. "Maybe I could grow some seaweed that could carry the key over here." She flicked her tail sharply. Ribbon seaweed started to grow on the ledge where the key was. It tangled around the key.

"It's working!" gasped Aurora.

"That's it, grow this way," muttered Harper as the seaweed pushed the key towards them. Then the key fell through the fronds.

"Flippers! I nearly had it!" cried Harper in frustration. She flicked her tail again and more ribbon seaweed grew up from the floor. Harper screwed up her face with concentration as she made the seaweed push the key towards them, but the seaweed was thin and slippery and could only move the key a little bit at a time.

"Keep trying!" said Millie, as the key moved at

the pace of an ancient sea snail.

This is all my fault, thought Lyla, slapping her tail down in frustration. *We need that key now!*

Suddenly the key started to rise into the air.

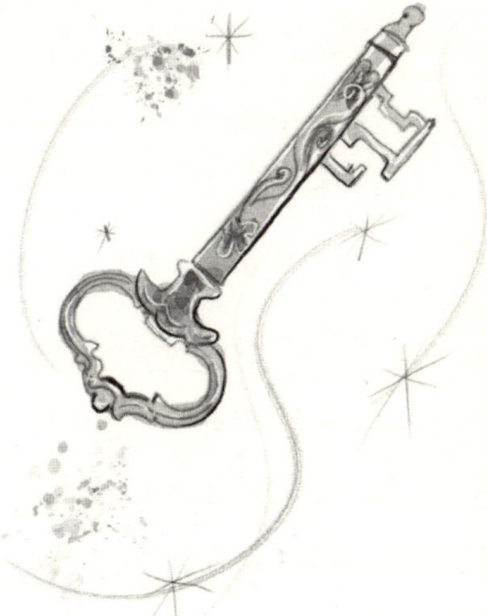

"What's happening?" gasped Millie. "Why's the key floating?"

"Are you doing it, Harper?" asked Aurora.

"Not me," said Harper in astonishment.

"I think it's Lyla!" Charm exclaimed.

Lyla became aware that all the scales on her tail were tingling and that she was feeling a strange connection to the key, as if a current of energy was flowing between them. She stared at the key as it hovered above the ground. "Charm's right!"

she breathed. She imagined using the energy to pull the key towards her and it began to move through the water towards the dungeon door.

"Lyla!" cried Millie. "You've got moving magic!"

Not daring to look away from the key, Lyla willed it to keep floating towards them.

CHAPTER SEVEN

The key floated through the bars of the dungeon and Lyla grabbed it. The strange sensation of energy connecting her and the key vanished and her scales stopped tingling. A sudden wave of tiredness overwhelmed her. But the key was in her hand!

Her friends erupted around her.

"Lyla! You found your magic!" cried Millie.

"Clattering clams! That's awesome!" gasped Harper.

"Now we can escape!" exclaimed Aurora.

The dolphins joined in with the congratulations,

whistling and clicking in excitement. Lyla could hardly believe it. Moving magic was powerful and very rare. She suddenly remembered the boulder falling at the wildlife reef earlier and the rock that had mysteriously risen in the water before bouncing away when she and Charm had been playing manatee tag. They could have been early signs of her magic appearing.

Charm nuzzled Lyla. "Are you OK? You've gone very pale."

Lyla blinked, trying to take it all in. "I feel really tired."

"Doing magic can make you feel exhausted at first," Millie said.

Charm's sparkling dark eyes met hers. "Lyla, your magic is mer-mazing!"

Lyla hugged her.

"Let's get out of here," said Millie.

Fitting the key in the lock, Lyla turned it and

the dungeon door swung open.

"We're free!" whistled Splash.

He raced ahead with Harper but they stopped at the tunnel junction. "Which way, left or right?"

"Right, I think," said Millie, just as Lyla thought *Left*.

Lyla opened her mouth. She was sure they should go left, but what if she was wrong and got them all recaptured? She was just trying to pluck up the courage to speak when Harper pounced on something on the floor a little way along the right-hand tunnel.

"Check this out!" She held up a jewelled stud triumphantly. "That merman had studs in his ears and tail. I bet this fell out as he left us. You're right, Mils. It is this way!"

Lyla felt a flicker of surprise. This way really didn't feel correct to her. But maybe Spiky Hair *had* lost a stud here?

She followed the others but her unease grew. This tunnel didn't look familiar at all.

Charm nudged her. "Cheer up, Lyla. Hopefully we'll be out of here soon."

"I think we're going the wrong way," she whispered.

Charm stared. "Say something to the others then."

"But I might not be right," fretted Lyla. "Millie and Harper seemed sure it was this way."

"You should still speak up," said Charm. But Lyla shook her head.

They swam on. The further they went the more certain Lyla was that they were going in completely the wrong direction.

They reached a junction. "I wonder which way it is now?" Millie said.

"I don't remember either of these tunnels," said Harper.

"Are we lost?" Aurora's voice quavered.

The dolphins whistled uneasily.

Charm nudged Lyla with her nose. "Lyla, tell the others what you've been thinking. Go on!"

Everyone turned to look at her.

Lyla's mouth felt dry. "I may be wrong… I don't know for sure but…" Charm nuzzled her encouragingly and Lyla rushed on. "I think we turned the wrong way back at the dungeon tunnel. We should have gone left, not right."

Her words fell into silence.

"But what about that stud I found on the ground?" said Harper.

"The merman could have dropped it another time," said Lyla.

"You mean, we really are lost?" Aurora said, her voice rising in panic.

"Flippers!" said Harper in dismay.

"Oh, Lyla! Why didn't you say something

sooner?" groaned Millie.

"I… I'm sorry. You and Harper just seemed so certain," said Lyla, feeling awful and wishing with all her heart that she had spoken out.

"What are we going to do?" said Harper.

"We could be wandering round here forever!" said Millie, pushing her hands through her hair.

"And we need to get out and breathe air," whistled Splash anxiously.

"We're all going to die down here!" cried Aurora.

"Wait!" Charm's voice cut through the rising panic. They all turned towards her. Charm's eyes met Lyla's. "Lyla, you can get us out, can't you?"

"Me?" Lyla squeaked.

"Yes," said Charm. "You've got a brilliant sense of direction. I bet you can find the way back to the dungeons and out of here."

Lyla took a deep breath. "I think I can

remember the way."

Millie grabbed her hands. "Then lead us! If we get back to the dungeon quickly enough, maybe we can still escape before the Mal Mer come back."

"Oh, please try," begged Aurora.

"But what if I get it wrong?" said Lyla anxiously.

"It's better to try than to not do anything," said Charm. She nuzzled Lyla. "You can find the way, Lyla. I know you can." Seeing the trust shining in her dark eyes, Lyla felt a new bubble of confidence swelling inside her. If Charm thought she could do it then maybe – just maybe – she could!

"OK, everyone," she said, surprised by the confidence in her voice. "Follow me!"

☆

It felt strange to have the others relying on her so completely, but whenever Lyla started to feel panicky, she glanced at Charm, who nodded encouragingly. Knowing that her dolphin trusted her helped her to push her worries away. With her confidence growing, Lyla sped up, and in no time at all they were back at the dungeon turning.

"Let's not stop," Millie urged. "We haven't got much time left to get out of the mansion before the Mal Mer return."

"We'll keep following you, Lyla," said Aurora.

"You're doing amazingly," Harper told her.

Lyla plunged on. *Left, right, right.* The tunnels all looked reassuringly familiar. She recognised the hole in the floor that looked like a shark bite, and the spotted lichen... *I'm doing it!* she thought with a flash of excitement. *I'm leading us out!*

But then, swimming round a corner, she came to an abrupt stop. Blocking their path was a bricked-up archway covered in green algae.

"Oh," said Millie, looking at the wall.

"Have we taken a wrong turning?" asked Aurora.

Lyla felt very confused. "I'm sure we haven't." She threw Charm an uncertain look, wondering what to do.

"Don't worry," Charm comforted her. "You must have made a mistake, but that's not a problem. You're doing brilliantly. Let's just go back to the last junction."

"But I'm sure I didn't make—" Lyla began.

Charm interrupted her. "Turn round, everyone!" she instructed, waving her flippers.

"Back to the last junction."

Everyone started to turn and Lyla made up her mind. Last time she'd thought she was right she hadn't trusted herself enough to speak up and they'd got into trouble. She wasn't going to let the same thing happen again. The Mal Mer's words echoed in her head: *You'll never get past our booby traps...*

Booby traps!

"Wait!" she said loudly. The others looked back.

"This *is* the right way," she insisted.

"It can't be," said Millie.

"We didn't swim through a wall to get to the dungeon, Lyla!" said Harper.

Lyla remembered the crashing sound they'd heard soon after the Mal Mer had left. Suddenly she felt even more certain she was right. "No, listen to me. I think this wall is meant to trick us. The Mal Mer said there were booby traps. I bet this wall opens. The Mal Mer closed it when they left to keep us trapped."

"I've read about trick walls," said Aurora thoughtfully, swimming to join her. "There's usually a hidden button or lever that makes the wall move. We just need to find it."

"Get searching, everyone!" cried Harper. She started randomly pressing bits of the wall while Millie and Aurora methodically checked one brick after another.

Lyla swam back and looked at the wall and the archway. The bricks the archway was made from were covered with green algae too. Her eyes snagged on one particular brick, halfway up on the left-hand side. It looked slightly different from the others. Why?

It's not as green, she realised. But why would that be?

Because hands touched it more often!

She raced to the brick and pressed it. With a crunching, crashing sound the wall slowly separated. The two halves slid back into hidden cavities in the archway.

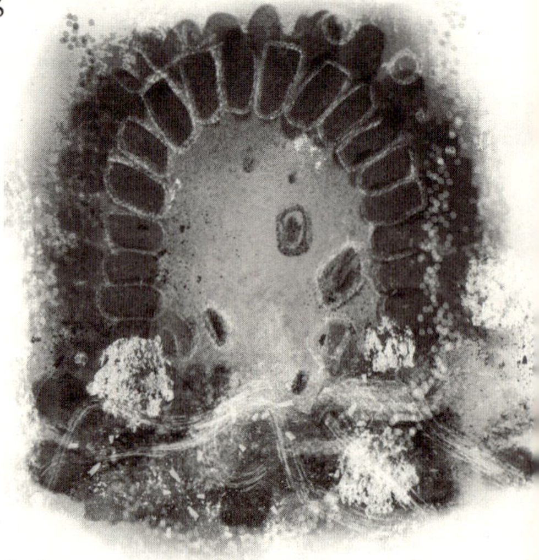

Harper and Millie whooped and Aurora hugged Lyla. "You were right! The wall was a trick!"

Lyla felt a rush of happiness. "Hurry!" she called, swimming through the archway and continuing on.

Left, right, right, she went.

They swam through the tunnel with the huge whale skeleton on the floor. Lyla remembered that the tunnel opened into a cave with bones on the ground, and relief flooded through her. They were close to getting out! But as she swam out of the tunnel, she stopped so quickly that Millie and Harper cannoned into her.

A very large spiny fish was swimming mechanically from one side of the cave to the other. Its large eyes glowed green and its mouth was open, showing rows of extremely sharp fang-like teeth!

CHAPTER EIGHT

Lyla tensed, waiting for the fish to look round and see them, but it just kept swimming from side to side.

"It's a bone snapper!" breathed Aurora. "They're very vicious and usually only found in the very deep sea. Because it's completely dark and mostly empty there, they evolved not to see or hear. They hunt by sensing movement in the water around them."

"What's it doing here?" said Millie.

"I bet the Mal Mer put it on guard to stop us getting out," said Lyla. "Look at its eyes. It's under their control."

"If we try not to disturb the water, maybe we can sneak past it," suggested Harper.

"I'll have a go," volunteered Splash.

"Wait, Splash!" Millie said quickly. "We don't know what it'll do if it senses you moving."

"I can use my magic to find out," said Lyla. She could feel her magic glowing inside her like a small sparkling ball of energy. She focused on it. Her scales started to tingle and she felt a force gathering in her fin. She flicked her tail and the energy shot out, making the little bones that littered the floor beneath the bone snapper jump and bounce about.

The bone snapper whipped round. Lyla heard her friends gasp as it dived swiftly at the bones on the floor and shredded them to smithereens. Then it rose back up in the water and began to slowly swim across the cave again, looking as if nothing had happened.

Lyla gulped. "Um... How are we going to get past that?"

"We can't. We'll have to find another way out," said Millie.

"But there might not be another way," said Lyla, thinking of the maze of tunnels they had been lost in before.

"We can't just stay down here forever. The dolphins have to go to the surface soon for air," Harper said. "If they don't..." Her voice trailed off. Without air, the dolphins would die.

Lyla's thoughts raced faster than a shoal of zebra fish. Millie's ink-cloud magic was no use –

the bone snapper wouldn't care if it was plunged into darkness, and its teeth would easily shred any plants that Harper could grow.

Can I do something? Lyla thought.

She remembered the way the fish had attacked the little bones on the floor. It had kept biting them until they'd been completely shredded, which hadn't taken it very long. But what if the bones were much bigger…

"The whale skeleton!" she gasped.

The others looked confused.

"Stay here!" Lyla pointed at the side of the cave. "Be ready to swim to that tunnel on the other side." She grinned as she saw the astonished looks on their faces. She realised she sounded just like Millie when she was telling them what to do!

She dashed back into the tunnel and drew on the energy inside herself. She let it grow until it felt like it was going to explode out of her and then she swished her tail towards the whale skeleton. The bones shook for a moment and then the skeleton rose into the air. Lyla focused every bit of her concentration on it and made it float down the tunnel. It was exhausting but her magic was strong enough to push the skeleton through the water and into the cave. She stayed focused even when she heard her friends' gasps as the whale skeleton floated towards the bone snapper.

"Get ready to swim, everyone!" she called out.

Her magic started to waver and for a moment the skeleton stopped moving.

"Keep going, Lyla!" Charm whistled.

Lyla thought about Charm and the other dolphins and what would happen if they were trapped down here, or if the Mal Mer caught them and made them wear those horrible collars. Hot anger rushed through her, giving her magic a fierce boost. The whale shot towards the bone snapper. The fish sensed it – and attacked!

As it pounced on the whale skeleton and started shredding the bones, Lyla heard Millie shriek, "Go! Go!"

Glancing round, she saw her friends and the dolphins racing across the cave. Letting the whale drop to the floor, she shot after them, adrenaline surging through her and powering her on. They reached the far tunnel and dived inside.

Looking back, Lyla saw the bone snapper shred the last of the whale bones with its fangs and then rise up again to carry on swimming back and forth.

"You did it, Lyla!" Charm exclaimed as Millie, Harper and Aurora hugged her.

Lyla was so tired her tail was trembling, but she knew they mustn't stop. "Keep … going … everyone!" She panted. "Right, left, left. We're almost out."

"Got it!" said Millie. "I'll lead while you get your breath back. You shout if I go wrong."

"Lyla, hold on to my fin and I'll help you swim," said Charm.

Lyla grabbed hold of Charm's fin. As their energies linked, she felt Charm's strength flowing into her, chasing away her tiredness and giving her new energy. Soon she was able to swim by herself. They passed the pillars with the stone wolf eels and swam under the barnacle-encrusted portcullis before finally reaching the door that led into the mansion's hall. Lyla's spirits soared. Now all they had to do was get through it and out of the front door!

Millie opened the door a crack and peered out. "The coast's clear!" she whispered. "Come on!"

As they swam out, Lyla looked over at the spinning rainbow squid in its cage. It looked so sad and hopeless with its long arms drooping, the colours barely showing.

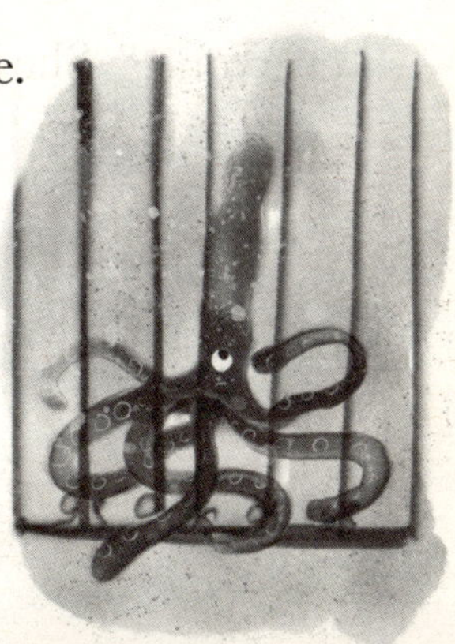

We can't leave it here, she thought.

She had already spotted a large key hanging on the back wall that looked just the right size for the lock on the cage. As the others swam towards the front door, she stopped.

"Lyla! Come on!" Millie hissed, looking round.

"No. We can't leave the squid here. We've got to set it free," said Lyla.

She gathered her power and flicked her tail at the key. Her magic lifted it up and it started to float past the cage towards her.

Suddenly a door at the side of the hall flew open. Lyla swung round. It was Spiky Hair and Silver Cloak!

"Our prisoners have escaped!" bellowed Spiky Hair.

"Stop them!" screeched Silver Cloak.

CHAPTER NINE

In her shock, Lyla lost control of her magic and the key clattered to the floor just outside the squid's cage. Millie fired a cloud of ink at the Mal Mer. "Swim!" she shouted to the others.

They turned, and for a moment Lyla thought they were going to be able to get away, but then the ink cloud vanished.

"Ink-eradicating potion!" crowed Silver Cloak triumphantly, holding up a vial of sparkling golden liquid. "We heard about your ink-cloud magic. One drop of this can disperse any ink cloud."

"You're going nowhere!" Spiky Hair's voice rang out. He pointed his trident, but Harper had slapped her tail down. The seaweed in the big planters at the sides of the room instantly grew, the spiky bushes shooting upwards, the sea vines racing across the floor and twining round the merman's tail. He tried to fight them off but they were coiling around his trident, pulling its prongs down to the ground. "Get off me," the merman shouted angrily. "Help!"

Lyla saw the mermaid narrow her eyes and aim her trident at Harper.

"No!" Lyla shouted, flicking her tail. She felt her magic rush at the trident, and its points started to lift up. It began to pull itself out of Silver Cloak's hands. She hung on grimly.

Lyla battled desperately to keep the magic going, but she was tired and she could feel her power fading. With an angry yell, Silver Cloak wrenched the trident down.

Swinging it round, Silver Cloak sent a blast of glowing green magic at the sea vines coiling around Spiky Hair. As the magic hit the vines, they exploded! Spiky Hair bellowed in triumph. Both Mal Mer pointed their tridents at the mermaids and dolphins, and advanced.

"You're going to be very sorry for trying to fight us," snarled Silver Cloak.

"We'll imprison you!" spat Spiky Hair.

"And keep you as pet mermaids," crowed Silver Cloak. "While your dolphins wear chaining collars and become our slaves."

"First, the dolphins!" cried Silver Cloak.

Lyla heard a faint grating sound but she didn't have time to work out what it was.

She and the others threw themselves in front of their dolphins, trying to shield them from the Mal Mer's magic. Lyla tensed, waiting for the magic to hit.

BANG!

The squid's cage door burst open and it spun into the room, its eight strong arms and two long tentacles twirling around it like a skirt. Its arms shone brightly.

"What… But how…?" Millie gasped.

Lyla realised that the end of one of the squid's arms was curled around the key. "It must have reached through the bars of the cage and got the key from the floor!" she cried. "It let itself out!"

The Mal Mer stared in horror as the squid spun towards them in a whirl of rainbow light. One tentacle grabbed Silver Cloak's trident while the other tentacle plucked up Spiky Hair's. Both tridents were hurled across the room and then the squid's strong arms wrapped around the Mal Mer. They yelled and fought wildly but they couldn't get away.

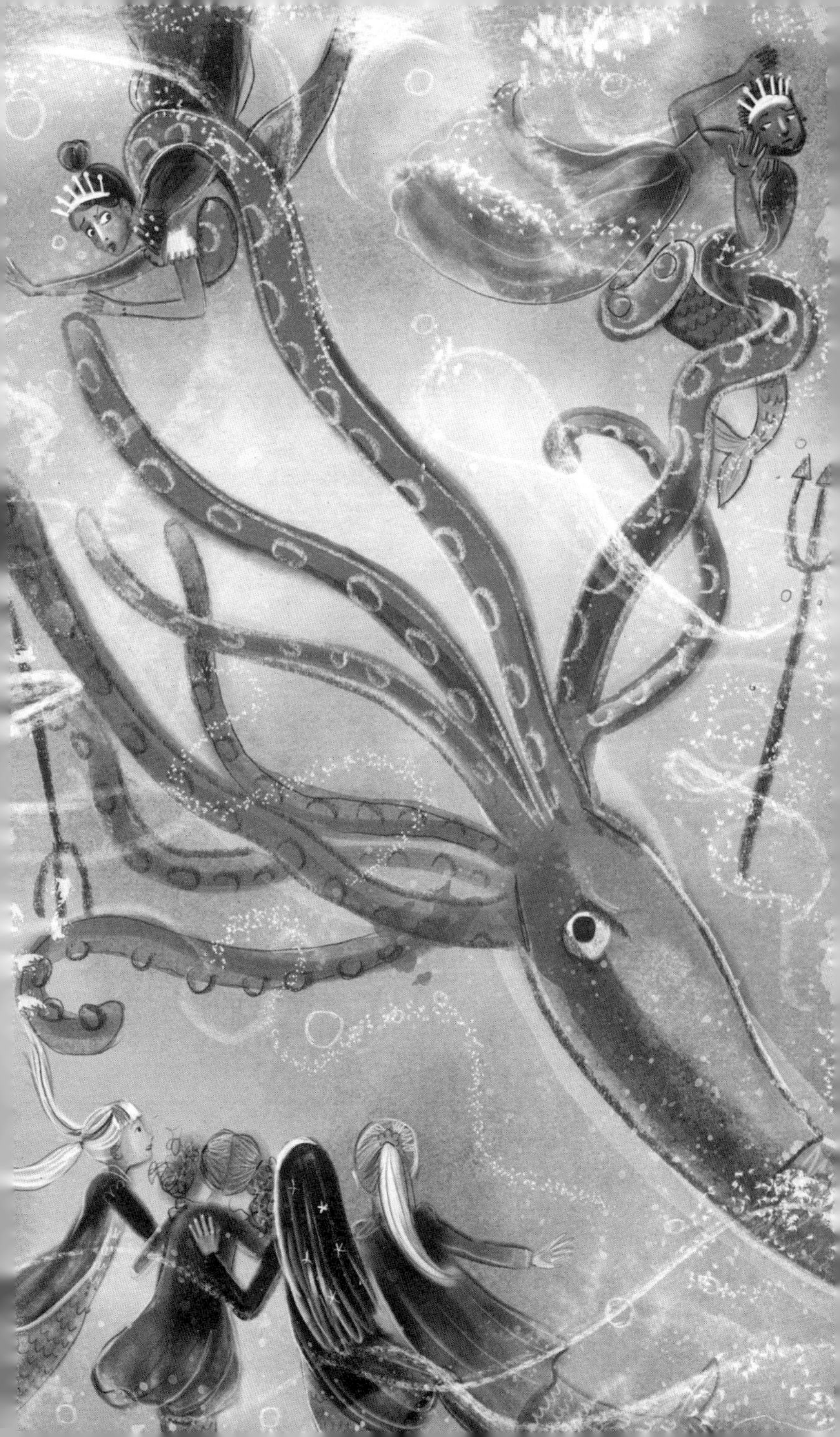

The Lilac Star mermaids and the dolphins hastily retreated to a safe distance and watched open-mouthed as the rainbow squid flung the two Mal Mer into its old cage and slammed the door shut. Lyla raced to the key that now lay on the floor and locked the cage door.

"NO!" shrieked the Mal Mer, shaking the bars of the cage. The squid's arms slowly lowered and it turned to face Lyla and her friends. The angry lights on its arms faded to a sparkling glow and it winked at them with one of its big dark eyes.

"Oh … my … wow!" breathed Lyla.

"Whizzing whales!" stammered Harper. "Or should I say spinning squids! That was awesome!"

The squid bobbed over to them. It was huge but, staring up at its kind eyes, Lyla didn't feel scared at all. "Thank you," she said softly, reaching out a hand.

The squid nodded as if to say *Thank YOU!* Then,

curling up the end of one of its arms, it fist-bumped her.

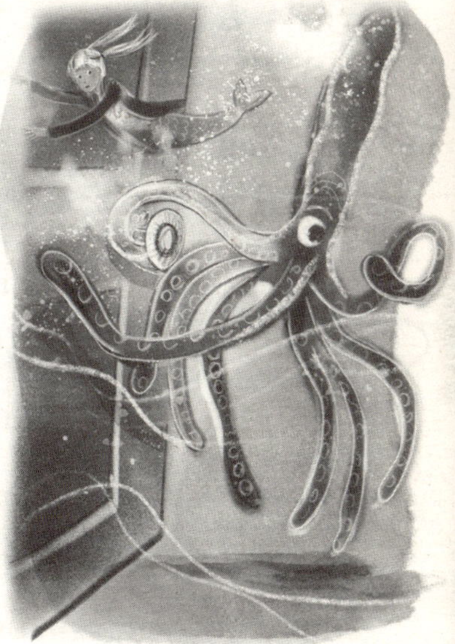

Lyla grinned. The squid reached past her and turned the handle of the big front door, pulling it open. It gestured to them to go through. Ignoring the furious shouts of the Mal Mer, everyone dived out of the mansion.

The giant squid's arms lit up with happiness at being free. It spun round three times and then shot away, leaving a river of bubbles in its wake.

"I can't believe we just got rescued by a squid!" Harper exclaimed.

"And we helped it escape too – or at least, Lyla did," said Millie. "What an incredible adventure!"

Harper grinned. "I think you mean ink-credible!"

Splash high-finned her as they all giggled.

"I'm just glad the squid is free now,' said Lyla, hugging Charm.

Aurora nodded. "No mer should ever keep creatures in cages." She shivered as she looked around at the empty, dead ocean. "This place is horrible. Can we go home?"

Millie nodded. "Bubble tunnels back to the loch, everyone."

They all swirled their tails and the entrance to four bubble tunnels appeared.

Lyla and Charm dived into theirs. They somersaulted in the frothy bubbles and shot out the other end into the cold waters of the northern loch. Lyla felt a rush of pure, heady relief. They were safe!

But as she opened her eyes, she saw to her

alarm that Ms Samphire was swimming towards them with the rest of the class behind her.

"Lilac Star!" Ms Samphire's voice rang out sharply. "I was about to organise a search party to look for you. Where in Neptune's name have you been?"

CHAPTER TEN

Remembering that after previous adventures Dr Oceania had asked Lilac Star not to mention their encounters with the Mal Mer, Lyla asked if they could talk to Ms Samphire alone. Ms Samphire agreed and took them to one side. All speaking at once, they began to tell her everything that had happened.

"Wait!" she said, holding up her hands after a few minutes. "Mal Mer? Dungeons? Booby traps? Dr Oceania needs to hear about this."

Ms Samphire created a giant bubble tunnel, called the year group together and transported everyone back to Mermaid Academy. Once there, she told the other first-years to go and eat their lunches and took Lilac Star to Dr Oceania's office.

Dr Oceania was having a meeting with Mr Nori, the Wildlife Studies teacher, but they broke off and listened as Lyla and the others told them about everything that had happened.

"A spinning rainbow squid helped you!" exclaimed Mr Nori. "They're incredibly rare. I've always wanted to see one."

"It was stunning," said Lyla. She smiled as she remembered the beautiful, kindly creature. "And really friendly."

"These Mal Mer must be stopped!" Ms Samphire said, turning to Dr Oceania. "Kidnapping students. Threatening their dolphins. Keeping sea life captive. Whatever will be next?"

"You're absolutely right," said Dr Oceania. "I shall tell the Mer Guard immediately." She shook her head. "I hate to think what would have happened if you hadn't managed to escape."

Lyla shivered and stroked Charm. She didn't want to think about that either.

"I am very glad you're all safe," said Ms Samphire.

"Safe but very hungry," said Harper. "It seems ages since breakfast."

Dr Oceania's face relaxed into a smile. "Well, I think you thoroughly deserve your lunch now. And, Lyla –" she nodded at Lyla's tail – "it looks like congratulations are in order."

Lyla glanced down at the top of her tail where the outline of a floating key could now be seen on her right hip. When a student discovered their magic powers, a symbol of the magic appeared in their scales. She grinned. "I've got moving magic."

"And..." Dr Oceania's eyes moved to her tail fin. Lyla followed her gaze and gasped in surprise. Her fin had changed colour and now had stripes of green, purple and gold! She looked at Charm, whose tail fin matched hers. "We've bonded!" she cried, grabbing Charm's flippers.

Charm whistled in delight and they spun round together.

Mr Nori chuckled. "You two have spent too much time with a spinning squid!"

Lyla and Charm broke apart, and their friends hugged them and exchanged high-fins. Lyla felt fizzy with happiness.

"Go and have some fun now, Lilac Star," said Dr Oceania. "Forget about the Mal Mer. The Mer Guard will deal with them."

Shooing everyone out of her office, Dr Oceania swam off with Mr Nori and Ms Samphire.

"Food!" exclaimed Harper, once they were in The Singing Circle.

Lyla perched on a stone bench. Patting it for the others to join her, she opened the bag given to her earlier by Ms Samphire and handed round the packed lunches. For a while there was a contented silence as everyone munched on seaweed pasties and kelp apples. When Lyla had finished, she sat back happily and admired the colours of her tail fin. Knowing she'd bonded with Charm was the perfect end to their adventure. Charm touched her matching fin to Lyla's.

"We're partners for life, Lyla," she said happily.

"I don't know what I'd do without you, Charm,"

Lyla said, meaning it. "You're mer-mazing!"

"You're the mer-mazing one," said Charm. "We'd never have escaped today if it wasn't for you. I was really proud of you for speaking out after I had told everyone to turn back at the wall. That took a lot of courage."

"I was only able to because of you. You were so confident when you told everyone that I could lead them out of the maze, it helped me to start believing in myself."

Charm nuzzled her. "You absolutely should believe in yourself."

Millie overheard. "Charm's right, Lyla. We wouldn't have got out of the maze if you hadn't remembered the way."

"Yes, and we couldn't have got past that wall if you hadn't remembered the Mal Mer talking about booby traps," put in Aurora.

"We'd never have got past the bone snapper

without you either," added Harper.

Lyla blushed. Part of her wanted to say that none of those things were particularly clever or special but as she thought about it, she realised that maybe they were pretty swishy.

Charm nuzzled her. "Before we went on the adventure, I thought we were perfect partners for each other because you don't like making decisions and I do. But when you insisted that we were in the right place by the trick wall, I realised that we'll be much stronger partners if you speak up more and I listen to you."

Lyla drew Charm to her in a hug. Had it been that moment by the wall when she and Charm had bonded? Or had it been even earlier, when Charm had trusted her to lead them out?

Charm kissed her nose, and Lyla giggled and kissed her back.

"Are you two done?" said Millie, rolling her

eyes, but she was smiling and her voice was warm. "Seriously, Lyla, Charm is right. If you have an idea, then we'd all like you to speak up. Your thoughts are definitely worth sharing."

"OK, I will." Lyla paused, remembering something that had been nagging at the back of her mind. She'd been wondering if it was important enough to share, but she remembered the lesson she'd learned today and said, "Did any of you think it was odd when the Mal Mer said they were going to find Wise Sage *and wake the sleeping beast*?"

"I'd forgotten that," said Millie. "It was weird."

Harper nodded. "Wise Sage isn't a sleeping beast."

"That's what I thought," said Lyla, glad her friends seemed to feel that it was a strange comment too.

"Maybe they weren't talking about Wise Sage,"

said Aurora thoughtfully. "Maybe it's another creature they've got plans for. Something that's asleep at the moment."

"Well, if they are planning on waking something, we'll stop them!" Millie vowed.

They all nodded.

Looking round at her friends, Lyla felt happiness bubble up from the tip of her tail to the top of her head. "I'm so glad I'm in Lilac Star with all of you."

"Lilac Star are the best!" said Harper. She grinned. "I vote we forget about the Mal Mer for now and challenge Sea Jets to a fin-ball match!"

"Yes, let's!" said Lyla eagerly.

"First we need to pack away," said Millie.

"Easy," said Lyla with a smile. With a wave of her tail, she sent the food wrappers and kelp apple cores into their bags. "All done!"

"Your magic's so swishy," said Harper. She

grabbed Splash's fin. "Race you all to the fin-ball pitch. Last one there is a dozy dory!"

Laughing and whooping, Lilac Star zoomed away together through the glittering turquoise water.